Yell & Tell

By Debi Pearl

Samuel Learns To Yell & Tell

Copyright © September 2010 by Debi Pearl

ISBN (Print): 978-1-61644-016-9
ISBN (eBook): 978-1-61644-032-9

Published by
No Greater Joy Ministries, Inc.
1000 Pearl Road
Pleasantville, TN 37033 USA

Written by Debi Pearl

Characters created by Debi Pearl
Illustrations by Benjamin Aprile
Painting by Michael Pearl
Layout by Lynne Hopwood

All scripture quotations are taken from the King James Holy Bible.

Samuel Learns To Yell & Tell may be purchased at a special discount for schools, universities, gifts, promotions, fund raising, or educational purposes. Licensing and rights agreements are available.

Printed in the United States of America

First Printing — September 2010
Second Printing — September 2012
Third Printing — January 2015
Fourth Printing— July 2016
Fifth Printing - January 2020

Requests for information should be addressed to:

No Greater Joy Ministries, Inc.
1000 Pearl Road
Pleasantville, TN 37033 USA
ngj@nogreaterjoy.org
www.nogreaterjoy.org

A No Greater Joy Ministries book

This book was inspired by my brave young friend

who was wise enough to yell and tell.

– *Debi*

www.yellandtellbooks.com

Listen, Samuel, my little man
It's time to learn God's written plan.
He has a book to teach us all
The things he did both GREAT and SMALL.

Trees and bees, flowers and the breeze
God made them all even the fleas.

He made your eyes to see the light.
And tells us always to do what's right.

He made your ears, your hands and feet
Your body strong, and food to eat.

Samuel dear, learn all you can
For someday you will be a man.
And what you learn,
and what you do
Is who and what
you'll grow into.

This is a simple lesson
But one you really need to know
It will help you to be ready
Now that you have begun to grow.

Most all the children around us
Are as nice as they can be,
But there are among the good kids
LOOKING just the same
Some really, really bad ones
But I don't know their names.

BUBba's
pan

RED
PAINT

5

You will know he is a bad boy
By the things he asks of you
When no one else is looking
And no one else can hear
He will ask to see your peepee
Or want to show you his.

Now you know my little Samuel
This is truly bad.
Even if he is your friend
It makes God very sad.

So, I ask you now, Samuel son
Will you think it's all in fun?
Will you stay,
or will you *RUN?*

I'll not stay and think it's fun
This evil that he's done.
When he says hush,

I'll *RUSH*,

RUSH,

RUSH

To tell his evil secret.

8

Today our lesson is strange indeed.
I'll tell you of God's enemy.

He often seems so very sweet
And you may think he's really neat
He comes with gifts and words that flatter
Knowing he will leave you *SADDER*.

Will you know him when he comes

Disguised like our best friend?

He swings you round

He brings you toys,

He wants to play with every boy.

He often sits you in his lap

And when Mom and Dad aren't watching

He softly touches you down there

Whispering that you like it.

Then he says, HUSH, Don't say a word.

It is our little secret

No one ever needs to know

Besides, no one would believe you.

How can you know, you're just a boy?

When he offers you lots of toys?

Will you do just as he says and keep his evil secret?

Or will you *RUN* and *TELL* and *YELL?*

Will you be brave, my Samuel?

I didn't know, little Samuel said,
An evil man might just pretend
To be our very special friend.

Now if he touches me like that
I'll know that he is bad.
I will not hush,
But I will rush and boy will he be mad.

I'll yell so loud and yell so long that
The table SHAKES and RUMBLES.
Then I'll run and tell and tell
I'll make that old pretender grumble.

Samuel dear, what if evil is a book

A book that's filled with nasty pages

Of strange unclothed ladies

And someone says, "Just take a little look."

Samuel, will YOU look
at the EVIL BOOK?

Will you dirty up your precious soul
With pictures that the devil took?

I know, the devil is a liar

He wants to spoil my soul

To dirty up my little mind

That's his final goal.

But someday soon I'll be a MAN

And be the head of a great big clan

What I see and what I know

Will determine how I lead them.

So I will not look at the nasty books
Nor at the pictures the devil took.

I know! I know! Just what I will do.

I'll yell so loud and yell so long

That the table SHAKES and RUMBLES

And then I'll run and tell and tell

Till his old books crumble.

But Samuel dear, I fear, I fear.

What if a **BIG SCARY BOY**

Pulls his pants down and says to you

Look at this, do what I say or you'll

Be hurt this very day.

What if he says, Don't say a word

Or you'll be very sorry.

Samuel dear, what will you do?

Will you be scared, too scared to yell?

Too scared to even, even tell?

I might be scared, little Samuel said,
But God is on my side.
So I will do what is right
I'll bring his evil deeds to light.

Don't you fear, Mama Dear
I'll do just like you say,
I'll YELL my very loudest
Even though he says be quiet.
Everyone will hear me
Everyone will know
I will defeat this evil foe.

Samuel dear, what will you do
When evil lures even you?

Someday when you think a nasty thought
Will you hide away so you'll not be caught?
Or will you stand for truth and light?
And do what you know is truly right?

Samuel dear, what will you do
When evil tempts *EVEN YOU?*

I will not hide, I will not cheat.

I will not *SLINK*,

or *SHRINK*

or *BLINK*.

And when evil thoughts come my way

I will pray, asking God to take them away

I will stand for truth and light.

I will fight with all my might.

I am ready now my Mama

I know just what I'll do

If someone touches my peepee

I will *ALWAYS TELL* and always yell.

Just like you taught me, mama

And you taught me very well.

I'll start right now

And say it plain,

You kids out there

Should LISTEN.

There is an awful ugly thing

That really might just happen.

It's really very simple

All you need to know

Is never keep a secret

When someone needs to be told.

So don't be embarrassed

JUST *TELL* IT LIKE IT IS!

Learn to

YELL

Always

TELL.

I do

And so can you.

Dear Mom and Dad,

A child predator loses his power when he loses his cover. This book is written to teach children and parents this critical fact. If all children knew that they would be heard and protected when they yelled and told, it would stop most predators from child hunting.

Your children need to know that they can come to you any time and any place, and that you are ready to listen and take action to protect them. They will not understand this naturally; it is your responsibility as a parent to effectively communicate this message.

Child predators are professionals.

Predators know how to lie, they know how to make a child look silly, and they know how to make you feel embarrassed for even suggesting that they might be guilty of such a repulsive thing. Your child, on the other hand, is a child. He will feel ashamed, fearful, and uncertain, because his young conscience cannot bear such an evil thing.

The predator is most likely your friend or relative.

Of the reported sexual assaults on children, 50 percent are by a friend of the family, with another 40 percent of the predators being a family member such as an uncle or even a grandfather. Only 10 percent of reported sexual assaults on children are by unknown individuals.

A child predator might use his own children as decoys.

You need to understand that predators of children usually appear quite normal. Chances are the predator is married and has a family. It is common for a predator to use his own children to draw other children into his friendly but sinister circle.

A child predator will cause you to appreciate him.

He is always happily willing to take your children for the day. He seems to have a gift with kids. He makes you want to believe in him, to like him, to appreciate him. You briefly wonder if he is not exactly straight, but the thought is so repulsive that you put these evil thoughts behind you. And besides, it is so nice to have someone take your kids for an afternoon. It is a woeful exchange: you get a few hours of blessed peace, while your sweet three-year-old daughter loses her innocence and starts a life of brokenness inflicted on her by this "friend."

A child predator knows how to make your child feel responsible and guilty, effectively guaranteeing his silence. Most parents get so shaken at the thought of their child being molested that they make the mistake of asking questions with such intensity that the child panics and shuts down. Since the predator has already blemished the child's soul and mind, these poor kids are likely to be too fearful to tell the truth even with gentle questioning.

A parent MUST be proactive.

You must learn to look and listen. Watch your child. Watch FOR your child. Take a cue from Samuel's mama and ask "what if" questions without making your child feel fearful that you are going be angry with him or her. Every few weeks read one of the *Yell & Tell* books aloud to your children.

Outmaneuver the Predator.

In an effort to alienate your child from you, the sexual predator will seek to make an "us and them" relationship with your child. Keep the pervert out of his game by creating an "us and them" team with your children first. Keep an open dialogue with your child on this subject, so he/she will talk with you as soon as he recognizes that he is being manipulated by a pervert in sheep's clothing. As the Scripture says, line upon line, here a little, there a little[1], talking about the possibility of one of "those" kinds of people confronting your child. Teach them that whether young or old, good friend or stranger, if anyone ever touches you or tries to show their privates, then come and tell.

A parent must be sacrificial.

Don't take the easy way out. Only leave your children with people that you are positive are walking in truth. Just to be safe, go to several people who have known the person the longest and ask plainly, "Can you think of any reason why my child should not stay with this person?"

Let yourself be known as an unforgiving bear if anyone should ever touch your child.

If there is a sexual predator in your circle of friends and family, and he hears you talking about warning your children, he will be reluctant to take a chance with your family.

And any predator that knows you are willing to go to the ends of the earth to see any child molester receive the full penalty of the law, even if he is your best friend or brother, then he will most likely avoid your child. Predators look for the most vulnerable.

Don't be the devil's advocate.

Most parents like to avoid bringing this ugly thing to the attention of their social world. They simply don't want their child known as one who has been used, so they hush-hush the matter. The predator counts on parents and victims keeping their mouths shut. He will walk carefully for a few months or a few years, and then he will find another victim. Would to God we would all learn to hate what God hates for the sake of the little ones.

Dress your child for safety.

As hideous as it seems, the pervert loves looking at the bottoms of tiny tots. Take caution to dress your little girl in fitting shorts under her dress, so as to thwart the sick peeping tom. Think about how normal men would respond to a woman in a short dress with her legs propped up showing her panties. Child predators are given a smorgasbord of lustful scenes on every playground and in most church services. It is a chilling thought. As child porn grows, so do the number of men who are lusting after small children. We must be proactive in dressing our vulnerable children.

Be wise, but not paranoid.

Most people are normal and are as horrified about child molestation as you are. The trouble is that perverts hide behind a normal-looking face.

God promises wisdom to those who ask[2]. This priceless gift is easy to receive. In this evil generation of ready child porn, your children need wise parents to safeguard them. So ask for wisdom; ask and ask again and keep receiving more and more.

Also, don't let your mind build tragedy where there is only peace. In other words, don't be paranoid, always seeing evil where none exists. Wisdom will help you discern when you need to be concerned.

Most child molesters live out their lives in peace and success. No one ever tells on them, so no one ever knows except the silent broken trail of victims they leave behind. They feel safe because of all the children they have violated and not one has ever spoken out, even those that are now grown.

But someday there will surely be a day of judgment[3], when every perverse hunger they ever had will be revealed, and they will face the terror of an angry God. I will be there watching, and I will rejoice when their calamity cometh.

Until that blessed day, read this book and the other *Yell & Tell* books to your children. Talk about what you learn. Ask questions. Watch for signs of fear or anxiety in your child concerning any friends or family. Our children are given to us to protect and nurture. They need us. And remember that *a child predator loses his power when he loses his cover.* Tell your children every day, "I love you and want to keep you safe, so always, always tell me anything that needs to be told. I will always, always listen."

[1]Isaiah 28:10 For precept must be upon precept, precept upon precept; line upon line, line upon line; here a little, and there a little...

[2]James 1:5 If any of you lack wisdom, let him ask of God, that giveth to all men liberally, and upbraideth not; and it shall be given him.

[3]Matthew 18:6 But whoso shall offend one of these little ones which believe in me, it were better for him that a millstone were hanged about his neck, and that he were drowned in the depth of the sea.

Mark 9:42 And whosoever shall offend one of these little ones that believe in me, it is better for him that a millstone were hanged about his neck, and he were cast into the sea.

Luke 17:2 It were better for him that a millstone were hanged about his neck, and he cast into the sea, than that he should offend one of these little ones.